Pictures by Eros Keith

Uncle Hugh

A FISHING STORY

By Rita Golden Gelman

and Warner Friedman

Harcourt   Brace   Jovanovich
New York and London

Requests for permission to make copies of any part of the work should be mailed to:
Permissions, Harcourt Brace Jovanovich, Inc., 757 Third Avenue, New York, N.Y. 10017
Printed in the United States of America

Library of Congress Cataloging in Publication Data
Gelman, Rita Golden.
    Uncle Hugh: A fishing story.
    SUMMARY: A young boy learns the joys of fishing from
his Scottish uncle and a legendary fish, both named
Uncle Hugh.
    [1. Fishing—Fiction]   I. Friedman, Warner, joint
author.   II. Keith, Eros.   III. Title.
PZ7.G2837Un   [E]   78–4918
ISBN 0-15-292789-1

First edition

B C D E

For Paula, Louis, Jan, and Mitch

Chapter One

He wasn't just any fish.
He was a trout.
And he wasn't just any trout.
He was the biggest trout anybody
had ever seen.
He lived in a quiet pool near the
big maple.
Tom called him Uncle Hugh.

Tom's real Uncle Hugh lived
across the sea in Scotland.
He was very smart.
Uncle Hugh the Fish was smart too.
The only one who had ever hooked
Uncle Hugh the Fish was
Mr. McCallister, Tom's dad.

Mr. McCallister didn't fish with worms
and grasshoppers as Tom did.
He fished with "flies."
Not real flies, but hooks that were
tied with bits of feathers and fur to
make them look like flies.

"Once you've caught a trout by
fly casting," Tom's dad used to say,
"you won't want to fish any other way."
Tom wanted a fly-casting rod.
"You've still got to grow up some,"
said Mr. McCallister.

Mr. McCallister loved to tell about the time he hooked Uncle Hugh.

"I was passing the pool when I saw the mayflies floating and flittering on the water.

"Then I saw that big fish gulping the bugs. My heartbeat quickened. I tied on a fly. I cast three times and let the fly go. It floated down to where the fish was feeding.

"There was a splash, and I felt a tug on my rod. When I pulled the rod back, my pole almost snapped.

"He shot toward the log.
I couldn't hold him back
without snapping my line.
I was stumbling and falling on the rocks.

"Suddenly, he came up out of the
water only six feet away, shaking and
tossing his head.
He spit out my fly and crashed down.
I stood there—water dripping
down my face.
I've never felt such a fish."

Tom loved the story.
But he was glad that the fish got away.
Tom thought of Uncle Hugh as a friend.

Some days, when Tom was sure no one was
around, he would talk to Uncle Hugh.
"Dad says I'm not old enough to
fly-cast," said Tom one day.
"I wonder what 'old enough' is,
Uncle Hugh."

Sometimes, while Tom was sitting there,
Uncle Hugh would come out from under his
log and race around the edge of the pool.

Chapter Two

The real Uncle Hugh was coming
all the way from Scotland!
Tom had heard so much about him.
Tom could feel his heart pounding
as Uncle Hugh's train pulled into the station.

As soon as the man stepped off the train,
Tom knew he was Uncle Hugh.
He looked just right.
Big and tall.
A gray beard.
A curved pipe.
Tom loved him on the spot.

After dinner that night, Uncle Hugh said to Tom,
"I hope you'll take me fishing tomorrow."
"I will," said Tom.
"And I'll show you the biggest fish
in the world."
"Biggest in the world?" said Uncle Hugh.
"That so?"

Then Uncle Hugh went to his suitcase.
He took out a bamboo fly rod.
"It belonged to my father," said Uncle Hugh.
"I've had it a good many years.
Now I'd like you to have it."
Tom could feel the tears in his eyes.
He climbed up on the chair and hugged
his Uncle Hugh.
"I'm still not sure you're old enough,"
said Tom's dad.

The next morning, just as
the sun was coming up,
Tom led Uncle Hugh to the pool.
They crouched down and
waited quietly.

Suddenly, they saw a long, dark shadow
starting to move.
The huge fish shot to the center
of the pool.
Then he raced around the edges
and disappeared.

"That fish is a monster," said Uncle Hugh.
"I've fished all over the world and
I've never seen a fish like that!"
"That's what everybody says," said Tom.

"If that old fish could talk,
I bet he'd have a lot to say," said Uncle Hugh.
"Well now, lad, let's go try that rod.
I'll come back here later."

They followed the stream to a spot
halfway up the hill.
Uncle Hugh showed Tom how to put
the rod together.
He showed him how to tie on the fly.

Then Uncle Hugh held the rod
in one hand.
He brought the rod forward and back,
whipping the fly farther and farther
out each time.
When he finally let the fly down,
it landed so softly, it barely
rippled the surface.
Never had Tom seen anyone cast
so beautifully.

On the next cast, a fish jumped
and grabbed the fly.
"Well, what have we here?" said Uncle Hugh.
"Be a good lad and net him for me, Tom."
Tom brought the trout up on shore in his net.
Uncle Hugh removed the hook.
He held the fish.

"How beautiful they are," said Uncle Hugh,
giving Tom the fish to put back in the water.
"We'll let it get a little bigger,"
he said.

They moved upstream.

Now it was Tom's turn.
He got into the water and started to cast.

"Easy, lad. Let the rod do it.
That's the way," called Uncle Hugh.
"Don't use all that energy, Tom.
Use your wrist, not your arm."

Suddenly, a trout struck Tom's fly.
Tom began to reel in the fish.
"No, Tom, don't reel him in.
He's too big," shouted Uncle Hugh.
"You'll break the line.

"You've got to go slowly.
Tire the fish out.
Give him some line.
Take your time.
Hold the rod high.

"That's it," called Uncle Hugh.
"He's getting tired now."

Tom's heart was beating wildly.
He tried to net the fish.
Every time he got close enough,
the fish would turn and swim away.
Then Tom had to give him line.

Finally, Tom landed the trout in his net.
It was the biggest fish he'd ever caught.

His father was right.
Catching a fish this way was exciting.

"That's a grand fish, and it will make a
grand lunch," said Uncle Hugh.
"Pack up, Tom.
I'm going on back to have a look
at that giant in the pool."
Uncle Hugh took a fly out of the fly box
and walked off with the rod.

Tom just sat and looked at his fish.

After a while, Tom started back.
As he got close to the big pool,
he heard Uncle Hugh talking.
"Well, my friend, that's five
perfect casts.
You're a mighty smart fish!"
"Uncle Hugh," said Tom, "you talk to fish!"
"Oh, lad, I do. I do," said Uncle Hugh.

"And I talk to trees and the wind.
But most of all, I talk to the river.
Sometimes I can feel the river in me.
I can feel the flow and pull of the stream.
It's a wonderful feeling, lad.
A wonderful feeling."

"I don't think I understand about
the river," said Tom.
"But I talk to the big fish.
And I call him . . .
I call him . . . Uncle Hugh."
"Well, my lad, I'm proud to have the
same name as such a fine fish."

"Uncle Hugh," said Tom,
"do you think he'll ever be caught?"
"When his time comes, Tom.
He'll be caught when his time comes."
"What do you mean, Uncle Hugh?" said Tom.
"When will his time come?"
"Ah," said Uncle Hugh.
"Nobody knows, lad.
Nobody knows . . . except the old fish himself."

Chapter Three

It was September.
The leaves were red and yellow and orange.
The air was crisp.
Uncle Hugh had long gone back to Scotland.
Tom opened his eyes.
The sun was just coming up.
He tried to go back to sleep, but something
made him get out of bed.

Tom got up and dressed.
He grabbed his rod and
ran all the way to the pool.
He tied the yellow fly on his line.
Uncle Hugh had said that the yellow
fly was a good one for the fall.
Tom made one cast.
The fly floated toward the log.
Suddenly, the big fish leaped up and
grabbed the fly.
He splashed down with such tremendous force
that Tom nearly lost his rod.

Tom got ready for a big fight.
He tightened his grip.
He started to give the fish line.
That was when Tom realized that Uncle Hugh
wasn't fighting any more.
He was just lying there.

Tom lifted the fish out of the water.
He removed the hook and put him
back into the pool.

But Uncle Hugh didn't swim.
He was dead.

Tom could feel the tears on his cheeks.
I think his time has come, he thought.

Tom lifted the big fish in his arms.
He could feel the wetness through his jacket.
He could feel the wind in his hair.
He thought about what his uncle had said about the
flow and pull of the stream.

Standing there, with the fish in his arms,
Tom felt as though the river were a part of him.
Now he understood.
It was a strange and wonderful feeling.